MY New Scooter!

A first experiences story

WHIZZ!

This book belongs to

....

THIS STORY HAS...

Hoot
Jessie's toy owl

Jessie
She lives with her mum, dad and Baby Archie

Archie
Jessie's baby brother

Jessie's mummy

Charlie
Jessie's friend

Patch
Charlie's toy bear

Charlie's mummy

Read more books in this series:

Little Lost Pup

Brave Little Fish

Silly Spaghetti

MY NEW SCOOTER!

A LAUGHING LOBSTER BOOK 978-1-914564-34-5

Published in Great Britain by Laughing Lobster, an imprint of Centum Publishing Ltd.
This edition published 2022.

1 3 5 7 9 10 8 6 4 2

Illustrations by Julia Seal.

Laughing Lobster, an imprint of Centum Publishing Ltd, 20 Devon Square, Newton Abbot, Devon, TQ12 2HR, UK. 9/10 Fenian St, Dublin 2, D02 RX24, Ireland.

books@centumpublishingltd.co.uk

LAUGHING LOBSTER, CENTUM PUBLISHING LIMITED Reg. No. 08497203

A CIP catalogue record for this book is available from the British Library.

Printed in China.

MY New Scooter!

A first experiences story

Let's play hide and seek! Can you find
Patch hiding in the story 12 times?

Jessie, Hoot and Baby Archie were going to Charlie's house with mum to play for the afternoon.

Jessie stood on her tippy toes and pressed the doorbell.
DING DONG!

A face wearing a helmet peeked around the door. "Hello!" said Charlie. "I've got a new scooter. It's red and I can go really fast on it!"

Charlie's mum opened the door and there stood Charlie – and his new scooter.
Jessie thought it was the best scooter she had **ever** seen. "Can I have a go?" she asked.

"Of course," said Charlie's mum.
"Why don't you play in the garden? I'll bring
a drink and a snack outside."
"Oooh yes!" cried Jessie. "We can play racing!"

Jessie climbed onto the step by the garden path and waved Hoot in the air. "On your marks … get set … **GO**!" she shouted.

Charlie scooted off as fast as he could. Round and round the garden he went, faster … and faster … and faster.

Jessie clapped her hands. "Can I have a turn?" she cried.
Charlie whizzed by. "Not yet!" he shouted.
"I think I can go even faster!"

WHIZZ!

So Jessie and Hoot sat down on the step to wait for a turn.

They waited . . .

and waited . . .

and waited . . .

. . . but Charlie still didn't stop.

"It's not fair!" said Jessie loudly. "I want a go!"

Just then, Charlie's mum came out into the garden.

"Hey, Mr Super-Speedy!" she laughed. "Isn't it Jessie's turn?"
Charlie felt his face go hot and red. "But it's **MY** scooter!" he cried. "And I want to ride it!"

"Why don't you have some juice while Charlie
finishes his turn?" suggested Jessie's mum.
So Jessie sat down to drink her juice while Charlie
scooted off. But she wouldn't watch Charlie. She was
far too cross!

Baby Archie picked up his beaker and waved
it at Jessie. "Juice!" he said happily.
But Jessie was even too cross to talk to Archie.

Archie looked at Jessie's angry face.
"AR-CHEE sad!" he announced. His bottom lip
began to wobble.

"What's wrong with Archie?" Jessie asked her mum.
"I think he needs cheering up," she replied.
"Why don't you play peek-a-boo with him?"

Suddenly, Jessie had an idea.
"I know how to cheer up Archie!" she said. "I've got a new game! It's called Hoot-a-boo!"

Jessie put Hoot in front of her face, then quickly pulled him away …
"PEEK-A-BOO! TWIT-TWOO!" she hooted.
Archie giggled. "Again! Again!" he cried.

Charlie heard Archie and Jessie laughing and stopped scooting.
"What are you playing?" he asked.
"Hoot-a-boo!" laughed Jessie's mum.

"Can I play too?" asked Charlie.
Jessie smiled and gave him Hoot. "We can take turns," she said. "It will be fun!"
Charlie blushed. He knew that Hoot was Jessie's special toy – just as special as his scooter.
"Thanks!" he said.

So Archie, Charlie and Jessie took turns playing Hoot-a-boo . . .

BOO!

Ha! Ha! Ha!

And Jessie was right.
It was lots of fun
taking turns!

Finally, Archie began to yawn.
"It's time for Archie's nap," said Jessie's mum.

"But it's Jessie's turn on my scooter now!" cried Charlie. Jessie's mum smiled. "Well, we don't want anyone to miss a turn!" she laughed. "Just five more minutes …"

"On your marks … get set … **GO**!"

THE END

CAN YOU REMEMBER?

What is Charlie's new toy?

 What is Jessie's favourite toy called?

Why does Jessie get upset?

What do Jessie and Charlie have to drink?

What game does Jessie play with Archie?

Does Charlie let Jessie have a go on his scooter in the end?

SAY GOODBYE TO...

Hoot
Jessie's toy owl

Jessie
She lives with her
mum, dad and
Baby Archie

Archie
Jessie's baby brother

Jessie's mummy

Charlie
Jessie's friend

Patch
Charlie's toy bear

Charlie's mummy

WHIZZ!

GOODBYE!